FERAL
TEETH
PRESS

De Mysteriis Ex Ultra

Feral Teeth Press

www.feralteethpress.com

ISBN:9780692696620

First Printing

Cover & Interior Illustrations:
by Mat Fitzsimmons

Should one wish to illuminate these pages, I would recommend using Prismacolor colored pencils to do so...

De Mysteriis Ex Ultra

By Mat Fitzsimmons

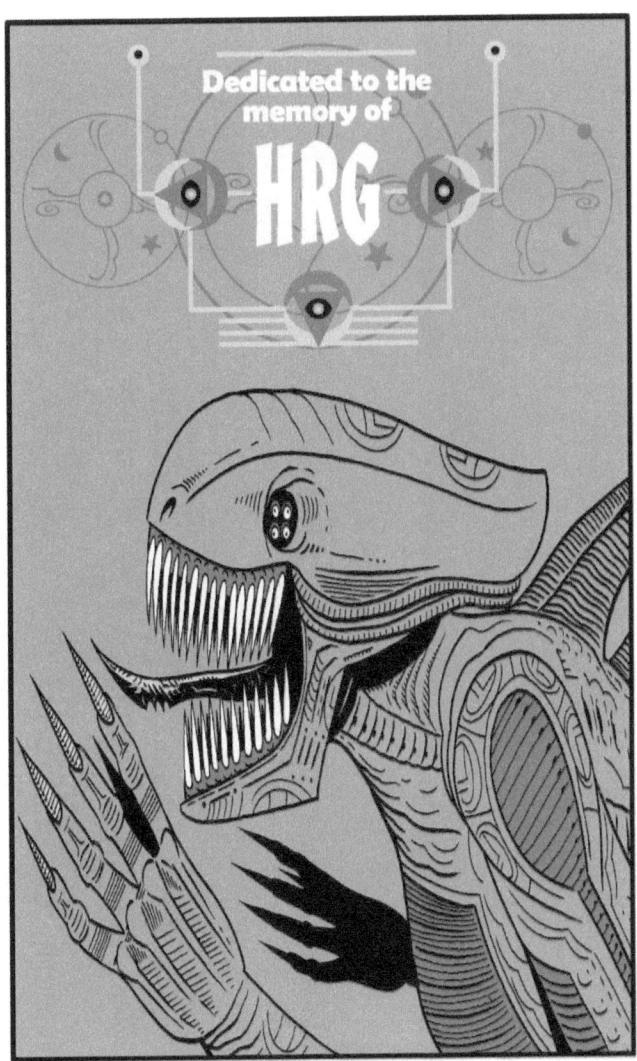

Dedicated to the memory of

HRG

The Greatest Teratologist of All Time

Before I am tried as a heretic, with the town's folk accusing me of being a Warlock, or, a Sorcerer, crying out with fervor that I be burned at the stake for the blasphemous things I've wrought in pen & ink; I only ask this one thing... Before I feel the heat upon my toes, or, until I'm held under water until I can no longer hold my breath; I ask you to first consider the works of Durer, Bosch, The Bruegels, Michelangelo, DaVinci, Goya, Gauguin, Beardsley, Dore, Picasso, Dali, Giger & Barker. For they, too, have conjured the Denizens of Hell...

One must prepare oneself, for an undertaking such as this. For 3 days, I had deprived myself utterly & completely of sleep, sustenance, all outside stimuli & all human contact. This had been a journey much, much longer in the making, though. Perhaps 2 decades; Since that first time that I'd slid through a—crack? —of the fabric of this dimension & into the fold of another. After floating amongst vast neon shapes, blazing blue in the blackness, larger than the mind could truly fathom; I'd snapped back into my mortal coil, trembling & shaking for perhaps 8 hours, maybe more, after my arrival back to our plane of existence. While floating through that other place, that dark dimension, I was vividly aware that these monumental shapes, geometrically abstract & glowing with a terrible, electricity-arc-blue, were sentient; Though they paid me no heed at all. I knew that, should anyone else encounter these things, they would consider them to be gods. Though, whether they were loving or indifferent gods, their intentions were not mine to know.

I eventually found myself dabbling in magic (a most dangerous past time). When I say magic, I'm not talking about your "sleight-of-hand", or Magic Shop variety; I'm talking about Ritual Magic; Invocation. So...this eventually, inevitably, lead to Crowley & The Golden Dawn. There was also a time, though I am ashamed to admit, I'd even browsed that charlatan, Anton LaVey's, catalogue. Rubbish!

It was while reading a text on Circle Magic, from the dawn of Ancient Hyboria, that I began meddling with Circle Magic. I had, up to this point, delved into the Tarot, the Ouija board & Mirror-gazing; But, I'd never tried making contact—calling up—an otherworldly entity before. That was what Circle Magic was most commonly used for, the calling of angels &...of other things.

After a length of time, years actually, along with a few slight modifications of my very own to this particular discipline of magic, I felt that I was ready to try & call up these creatures, the things that vibrate at different frequencies than we do...these beings that occupy the hidden nooks of deepest time & space. The things that crawled in inky netherworlds of a universe created from this Dark Matter; Something—a force—that is quite real, that mortal men (& women) are just now beginning to grasp. In my dreams, I have seen the equations for safely navigating black holes; for harnessing their dark energies. Though I dare not, lest I follow in the footsteps of a man who once said, "Now, I am become Death, the destroyer of worlds." Although, one only needs to turn the television on these days, to realize perhaps that's exactly what The Human Race deserves...

I would travel to those galaxies of eternal night, eternal darkness, if only to hoard the knowledge of realms unknown to mortal eyes; with exception of a very few, who have the strange ability to propel their soul-stuff, as did those of eldest Aegypt, out into the realms of the Dimensional Folds!

After cleansing first body, then mind & all which that entails, I began the preparations for an extended Drift. I played an album of strange, outré music; tribal in nature & heavy with drums & percussion. I burned a combination of herbs & oils in a censer, the heady smoke filling my small abode. I drank a liquor, which must be prepared precisely—the color of anti-freeze—before eventually nodding off into a state of extra-conscience-ness...what I liked to call The Drift...

I've made contact! In a dream, I was shown an equation, what I can only call...some kind of a Celestial Equation. These arcane equations were always numerical, far too complex for my brain to compute. The closest way in which I can explain these truths that I've learned is in the circles... The circles hide equations that house truths; Cosmic Truths! And it is only by understanding these truths, even if only in the realm of dream, that has somehow kept me safe & allowed my interactions with denizens of these interdimensional, nether-realms. The meaning & magic of these circles is always lost to me in my waking hours...The creation of the circles in this book are created in a trance-state, what I call The Post-Drift; though after drawing one of these circles, I always have weird dreams of swirling star-stuff, glowing with what I know to be the white hot heat of some alien radiation. It's this same heat that promises to burn the things I make contact with, should they cross the threshold of the equations I stand in, while out wandering those haunted & warped dimensions. And so, with the safety of this atomic light, burning in my mind & heart; I dare to wander the dark, so that people, fellow brothers & sisters of Humanity, may one day know what lurks between the folds in the fabric of our reality.

Though I must warn that one should not follow in my path, for it is dangerous & full of dread; unless, one is willing to invite a potential night visit from one of these creatures of Anti-Matter, from time to time. For, it is in the realm of dreams, that these things from these stygian realms, can still coalesce & take shape; coming closer to being something tangible; In dreams, they may still have substance! And to see is to know & to know is to call these strange entities forth. Without proper understanding of the circles, of the equations, I would not follow in my path, were I you... So I leave you, for now, with perhaps the soundest advice that a practicing magician may give another. Do not call up what you cannot put back down...

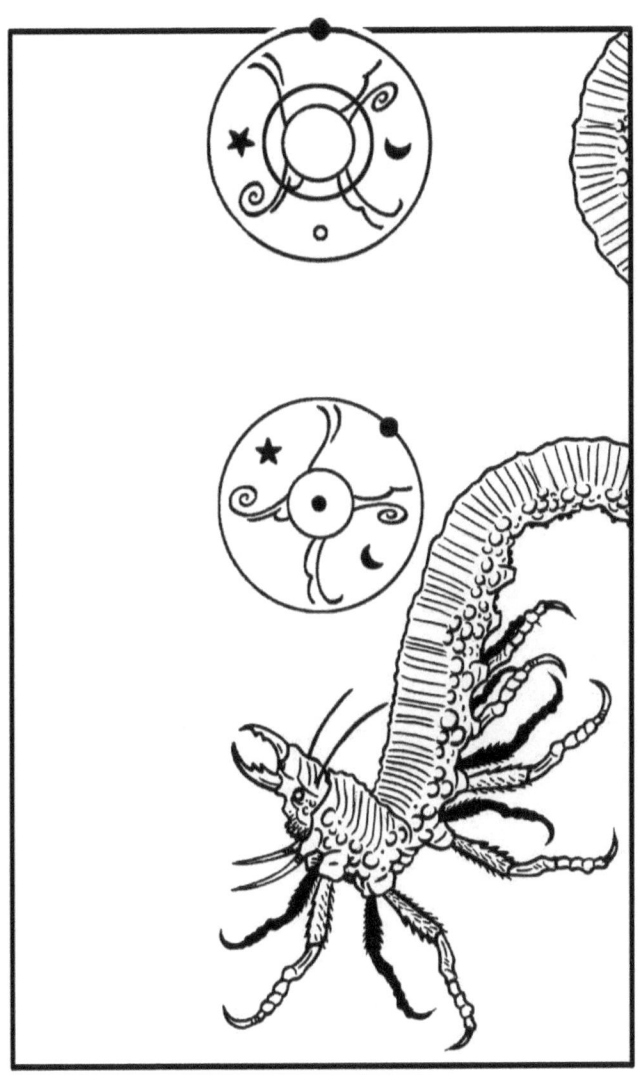

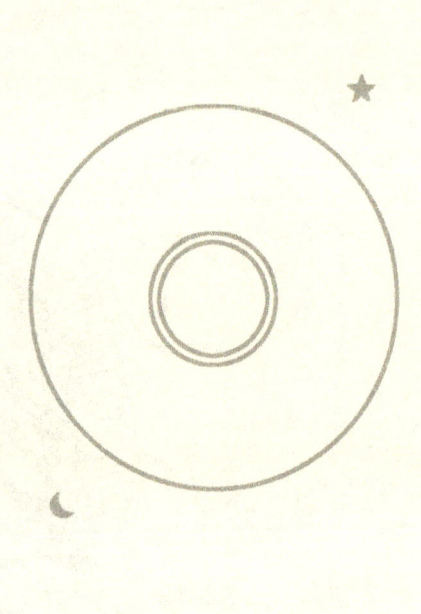

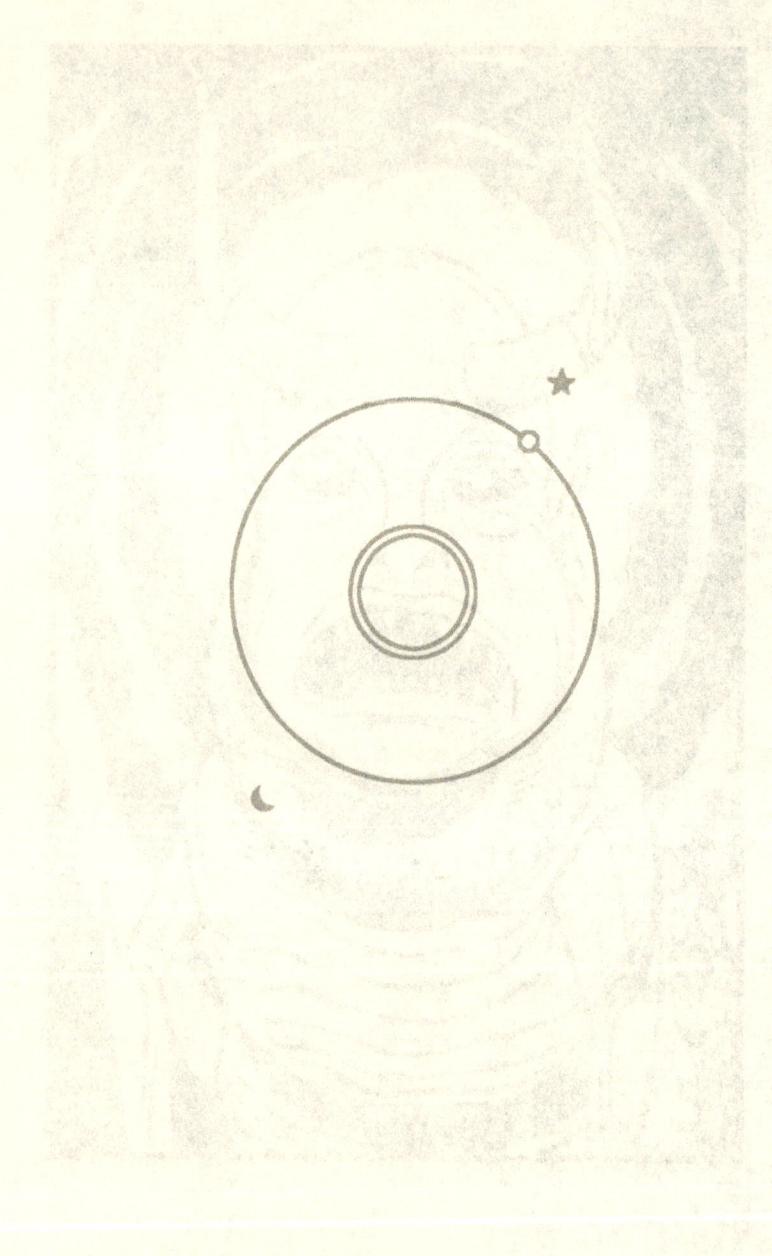

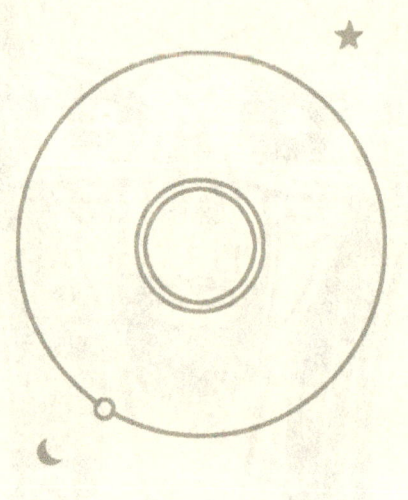

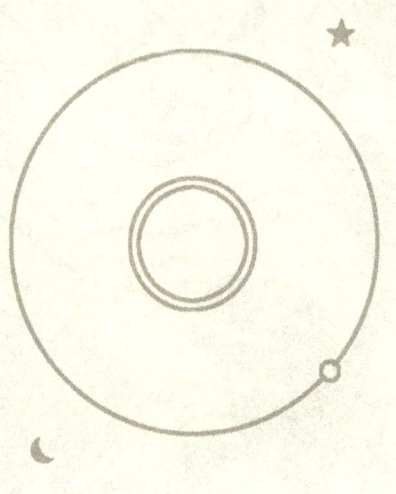

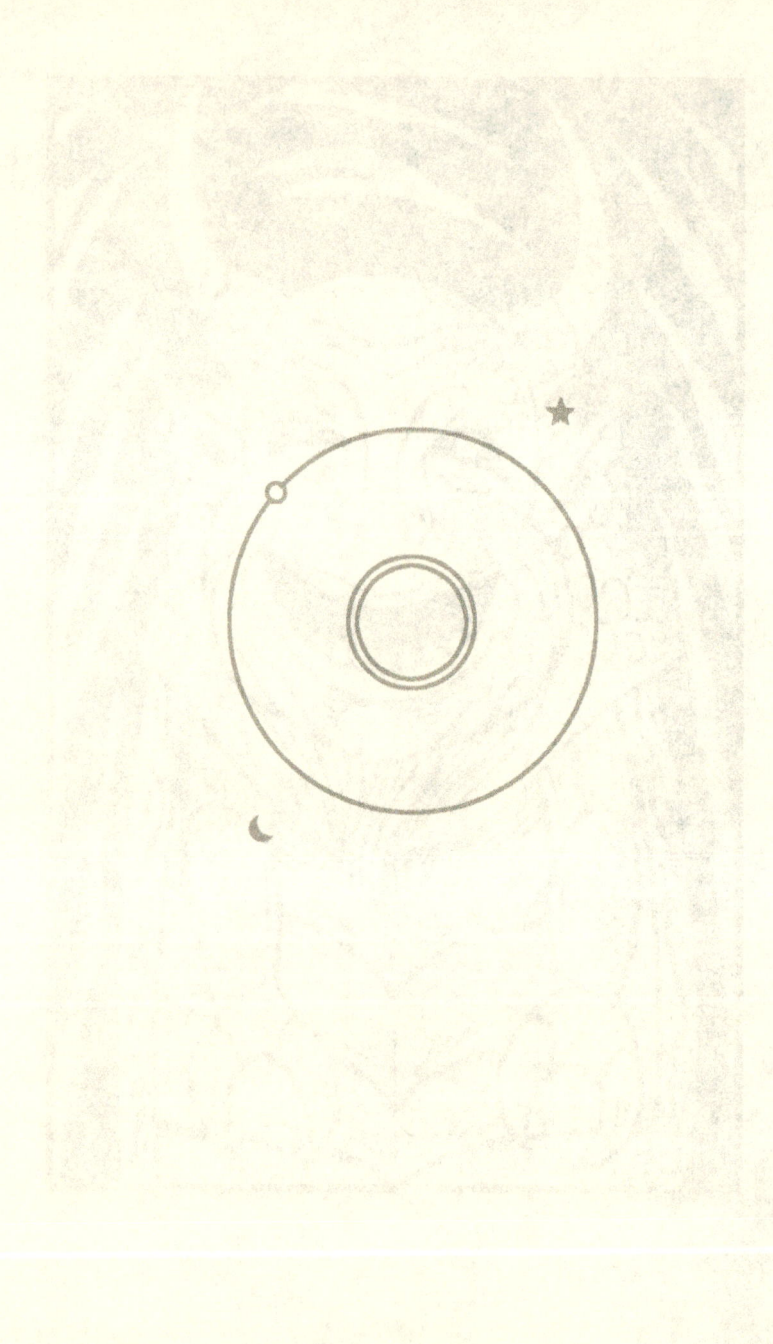

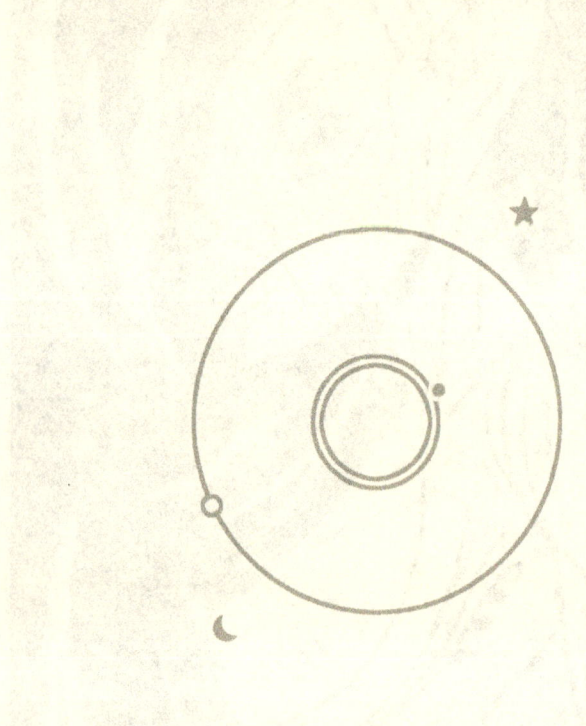

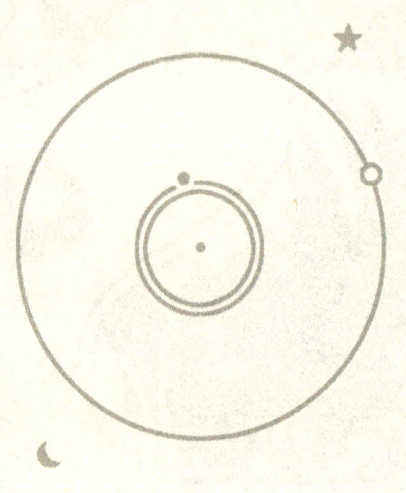

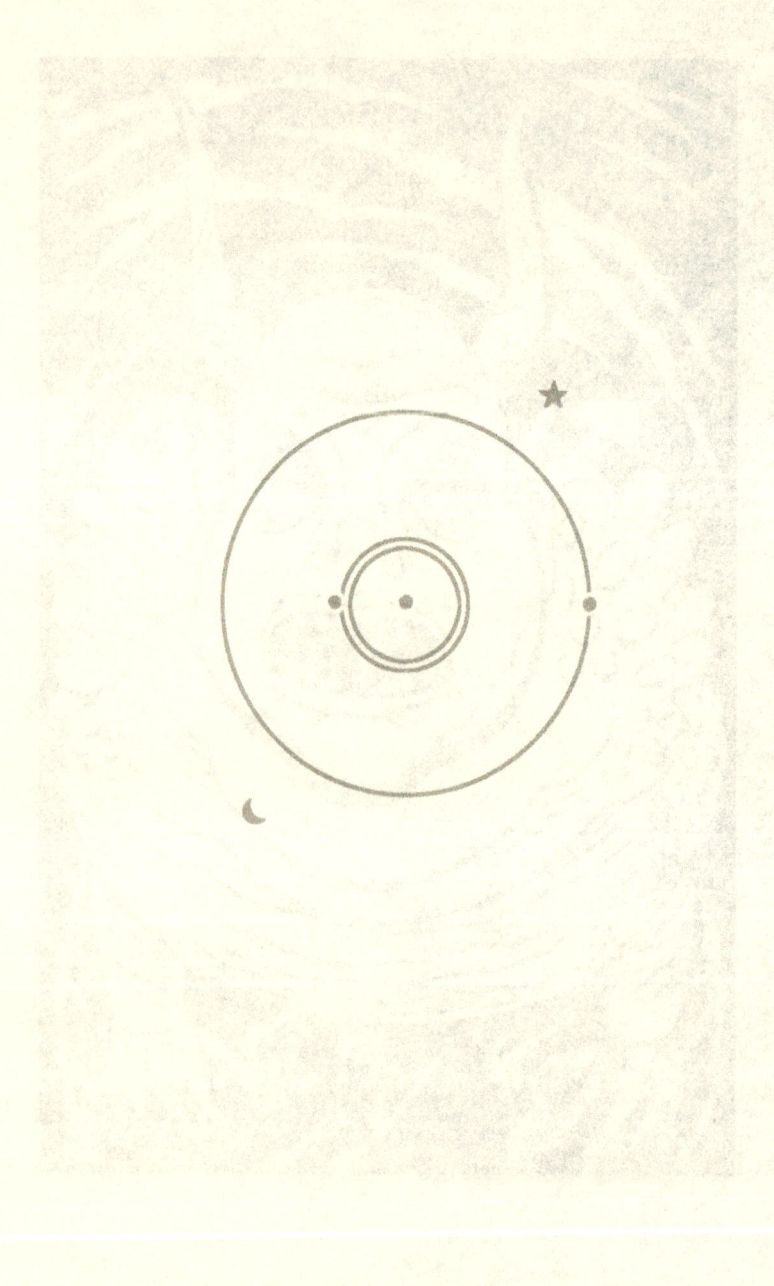

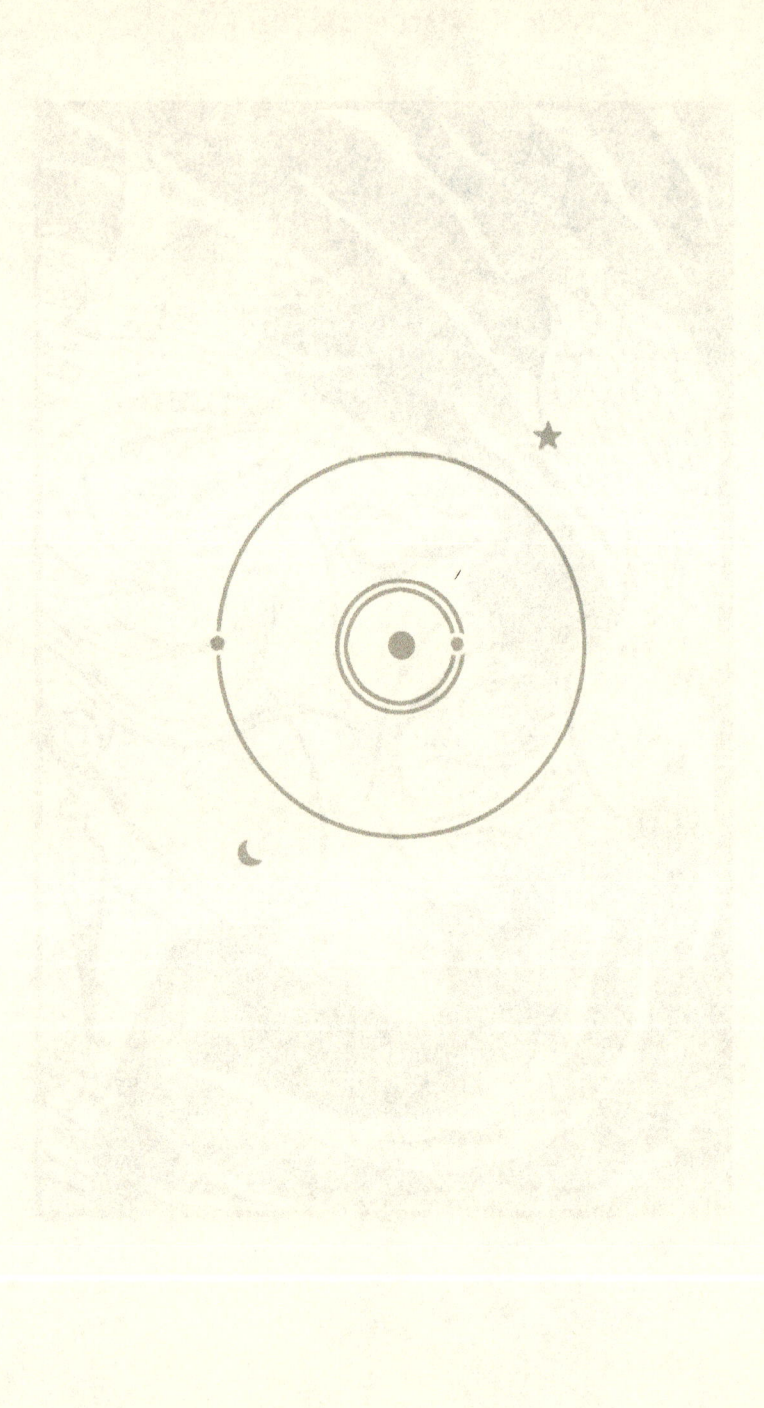

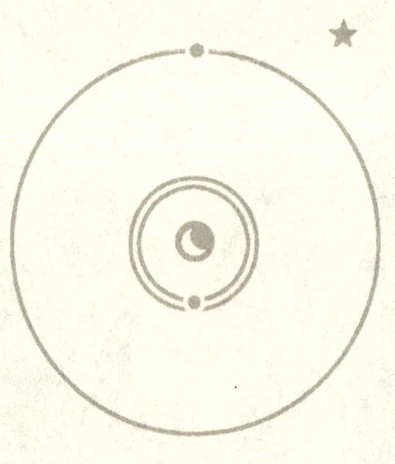

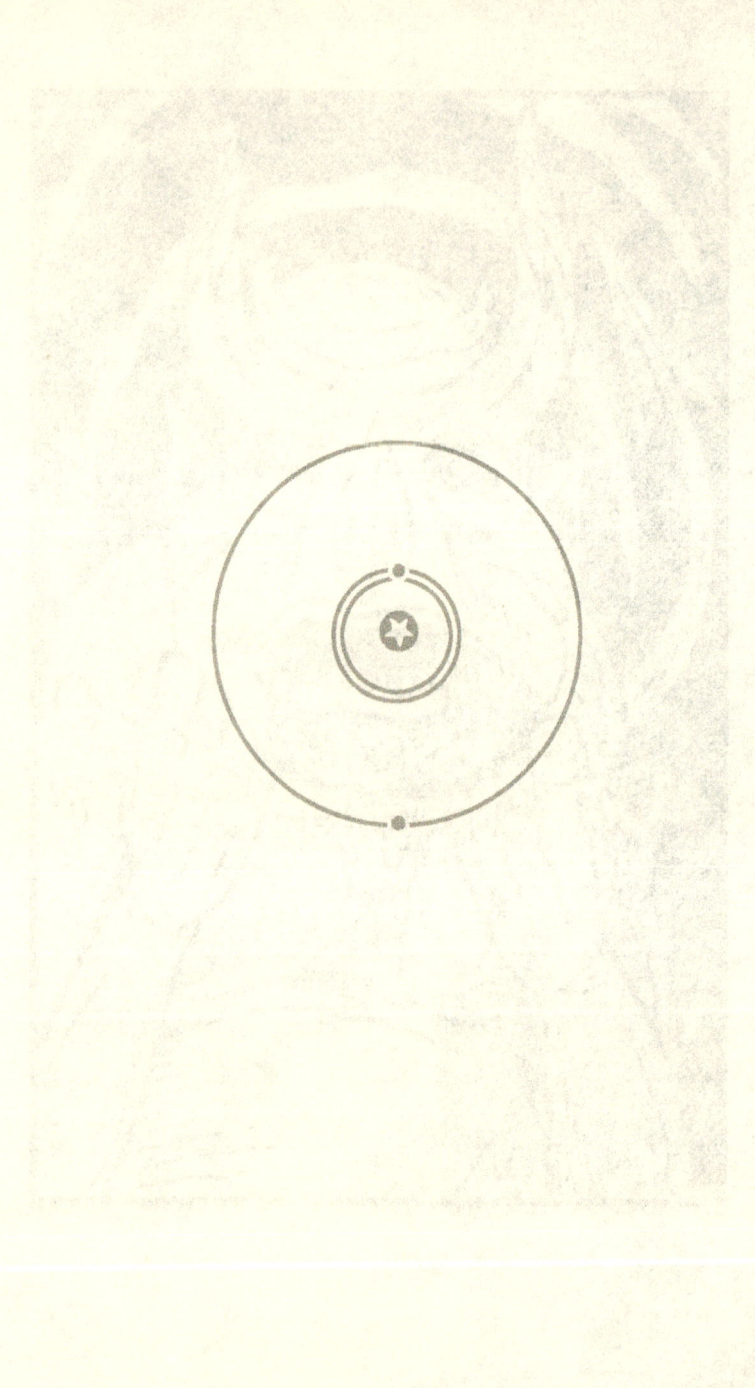

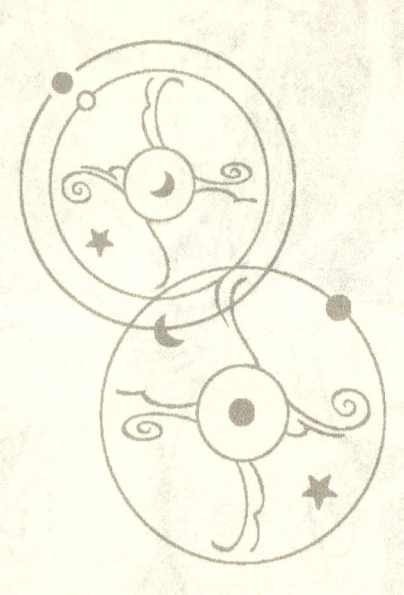

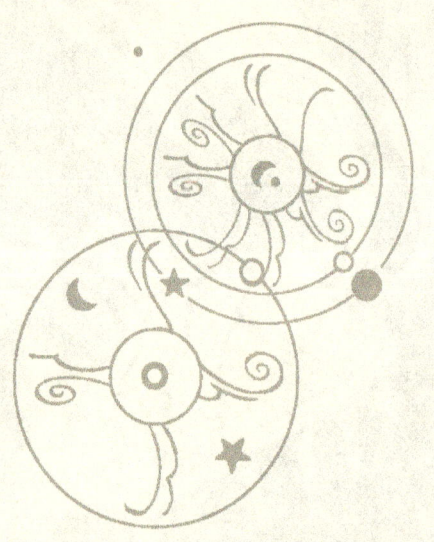

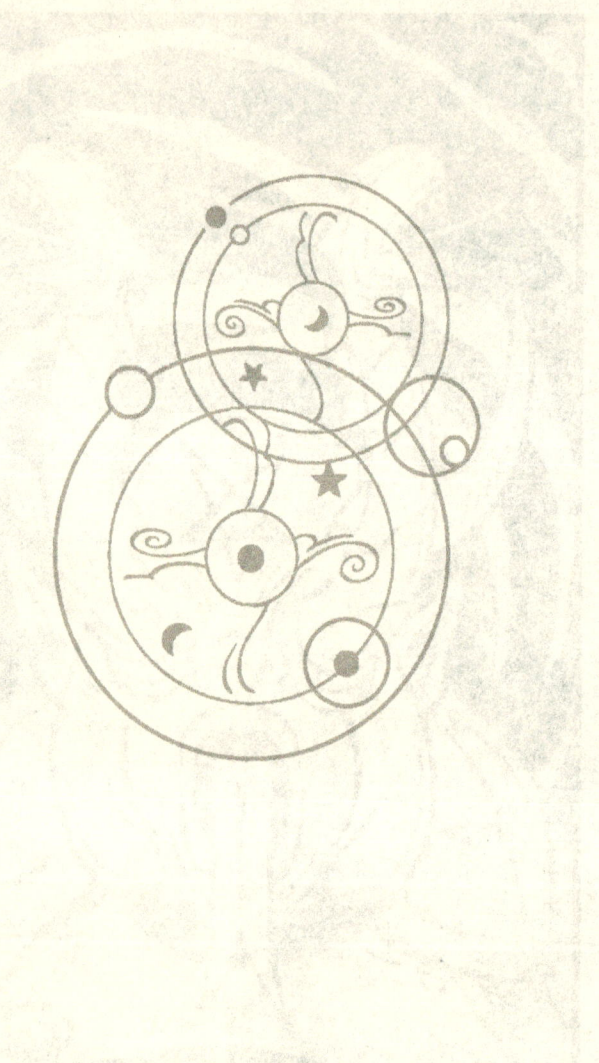

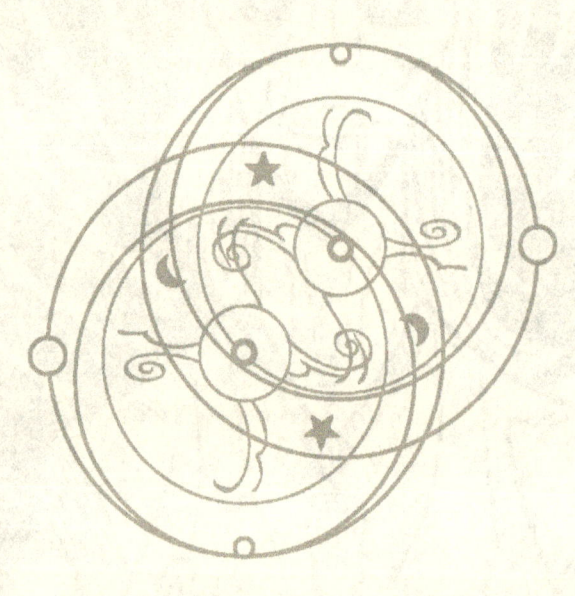

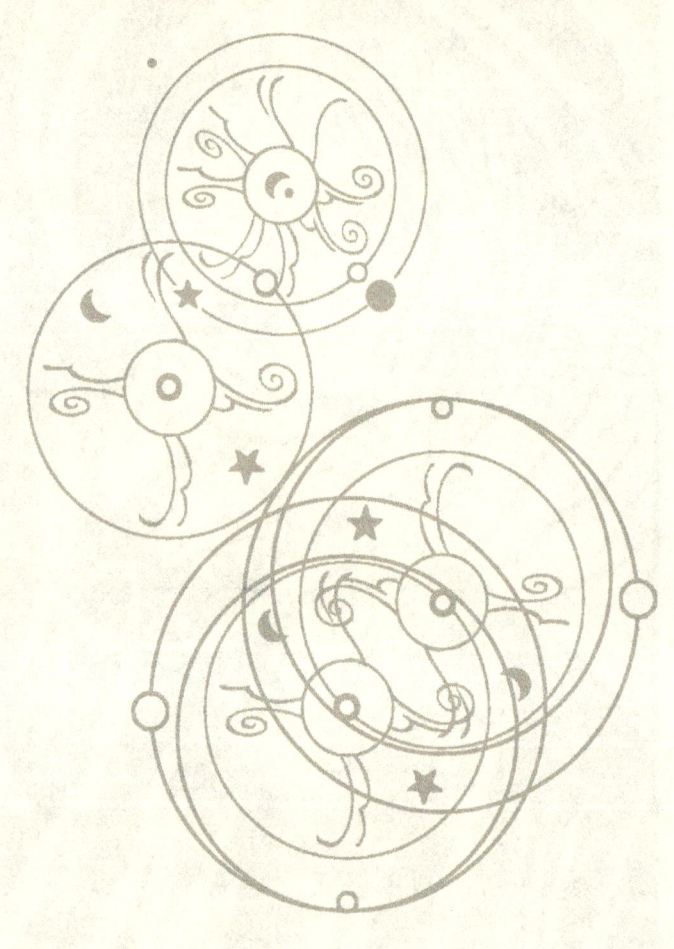

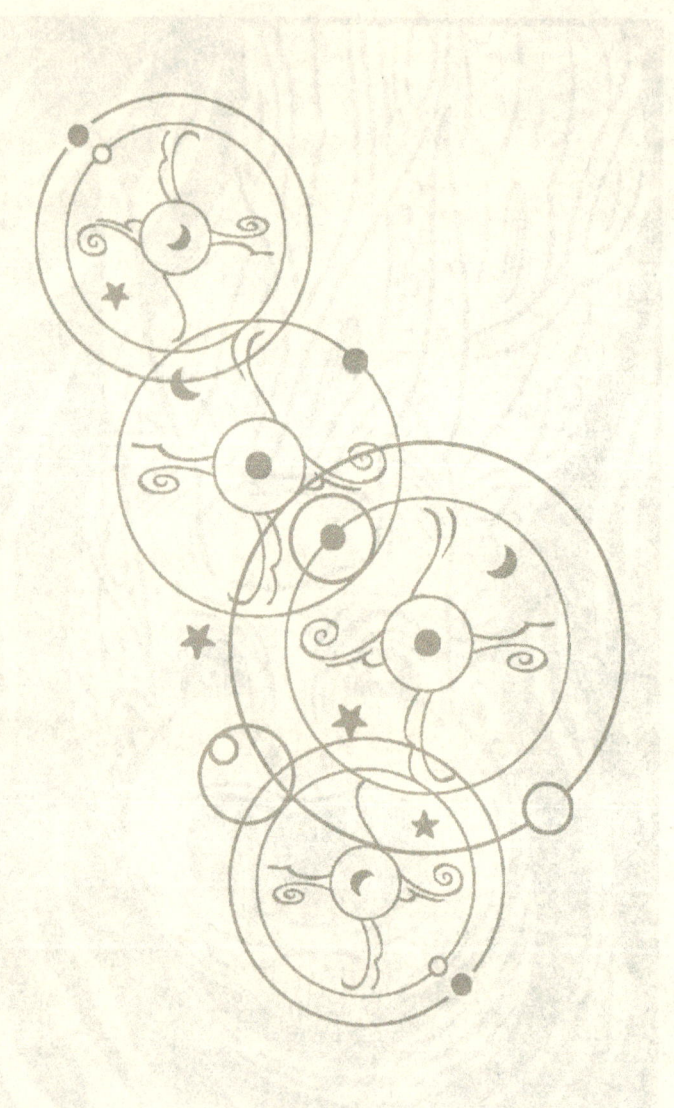

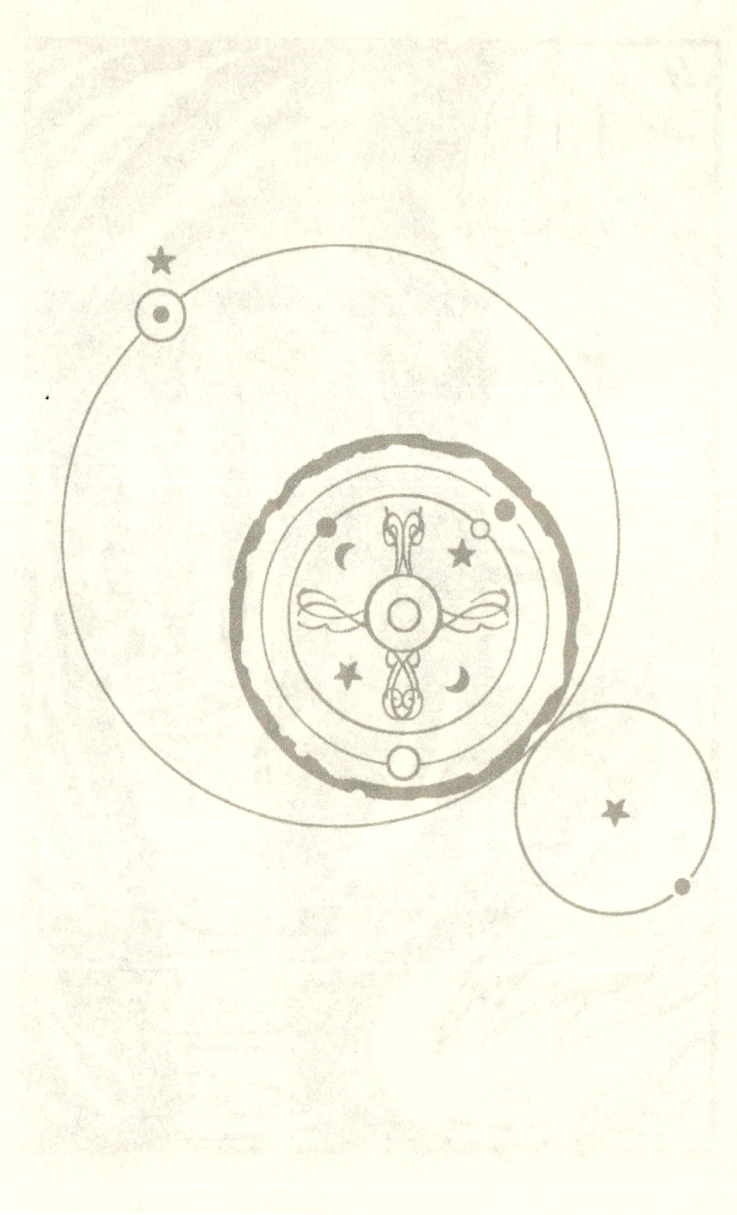

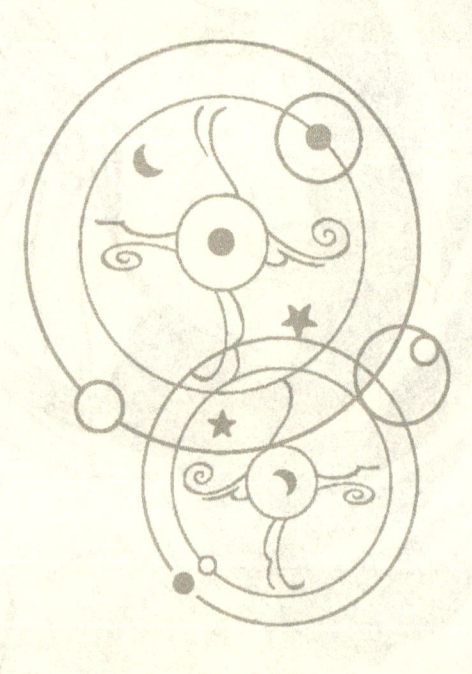

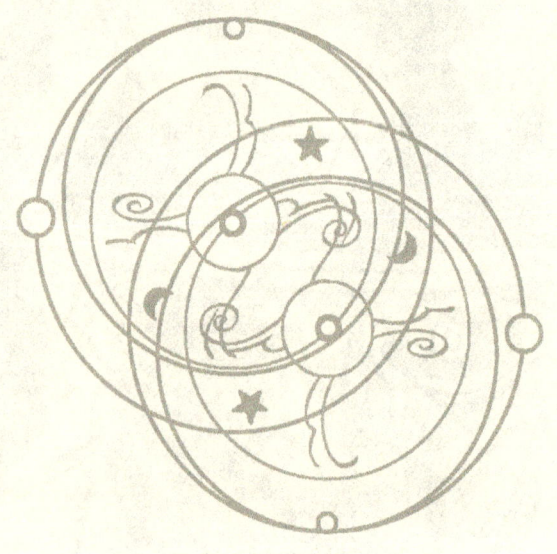

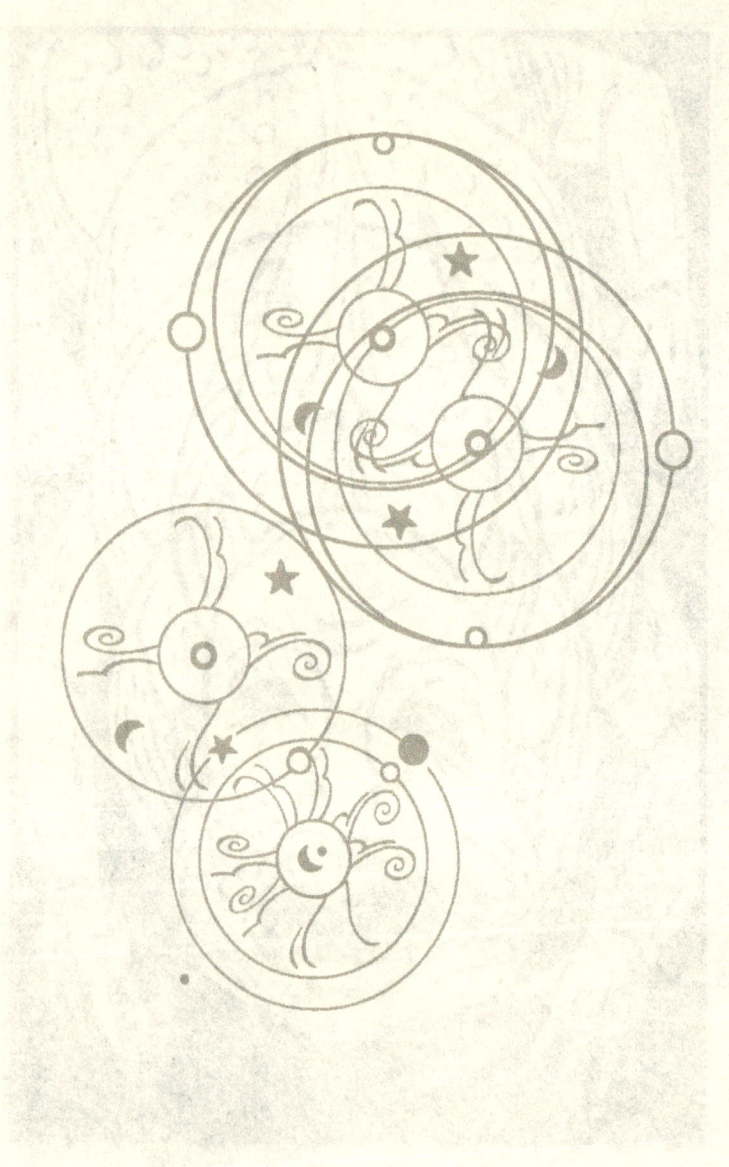

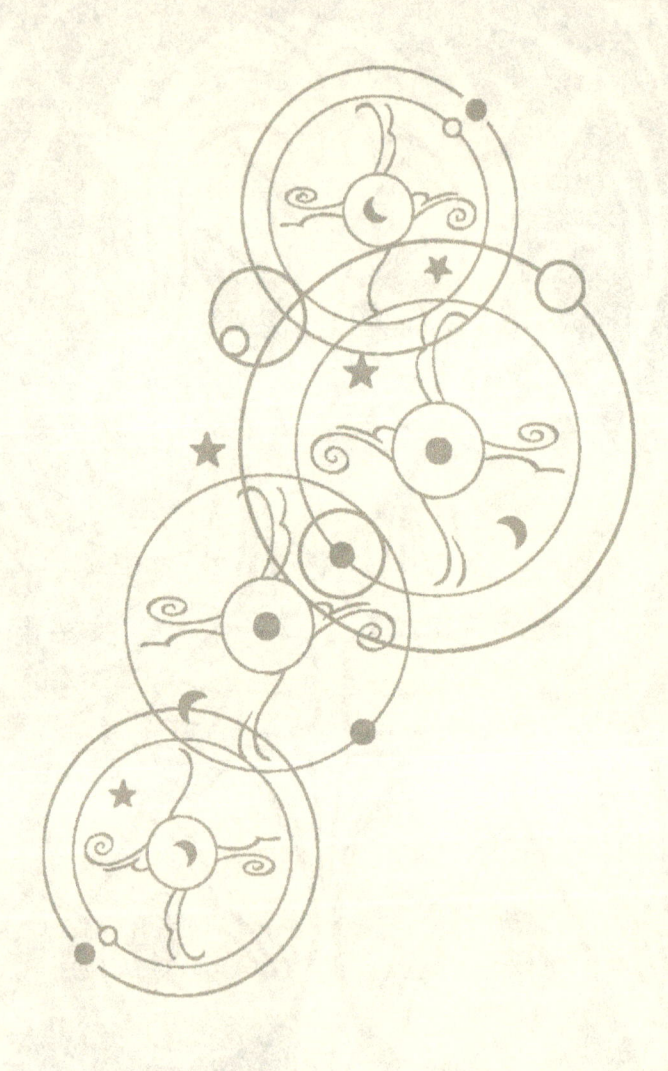

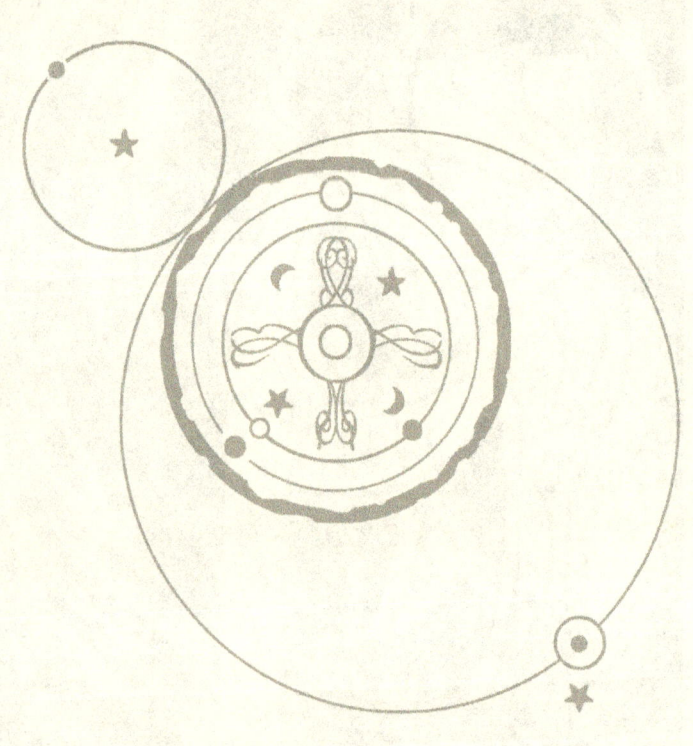

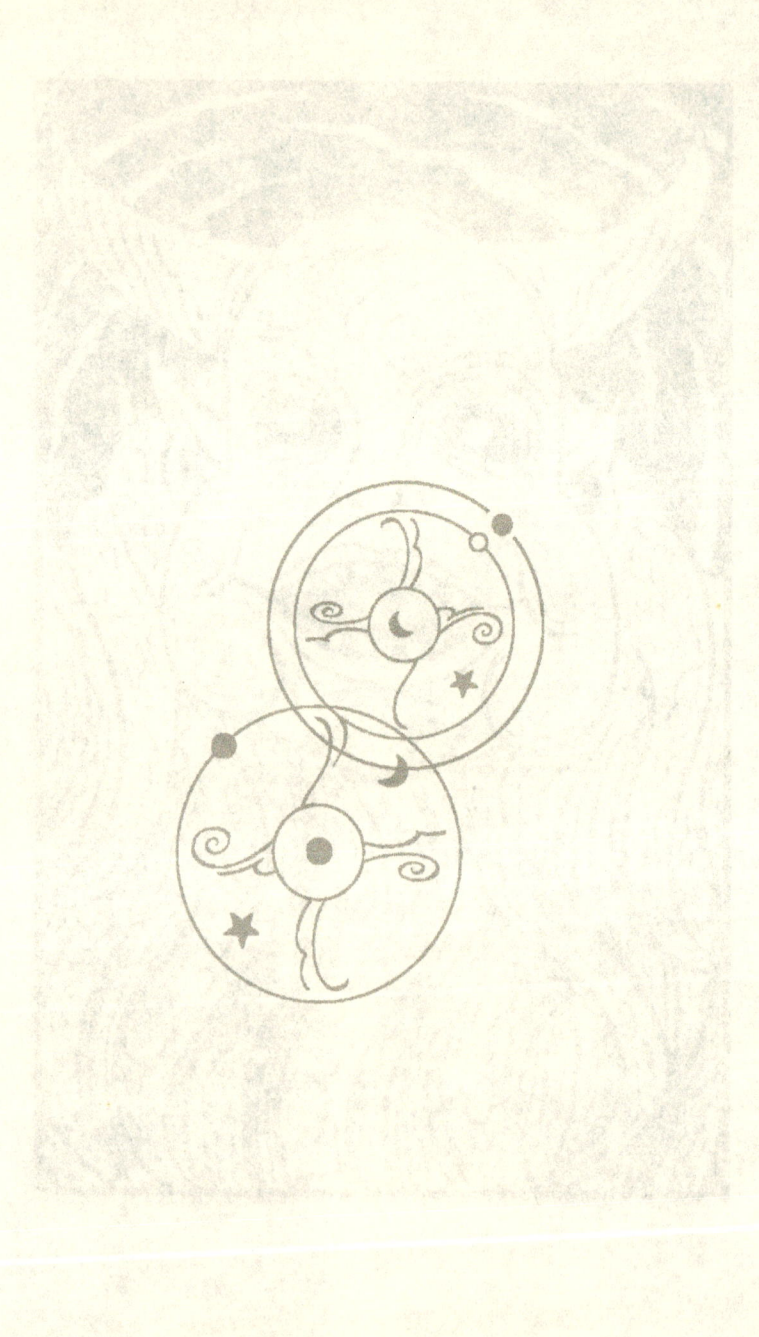

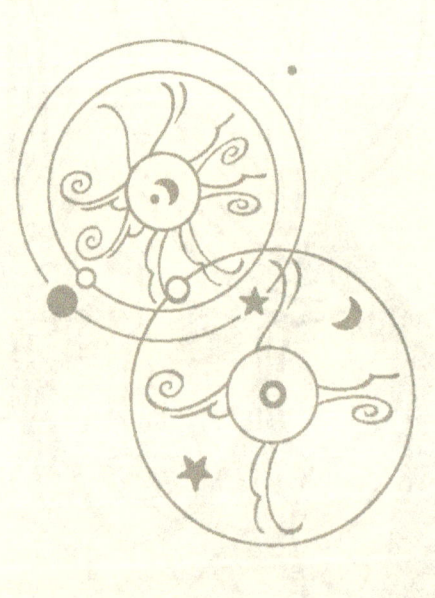

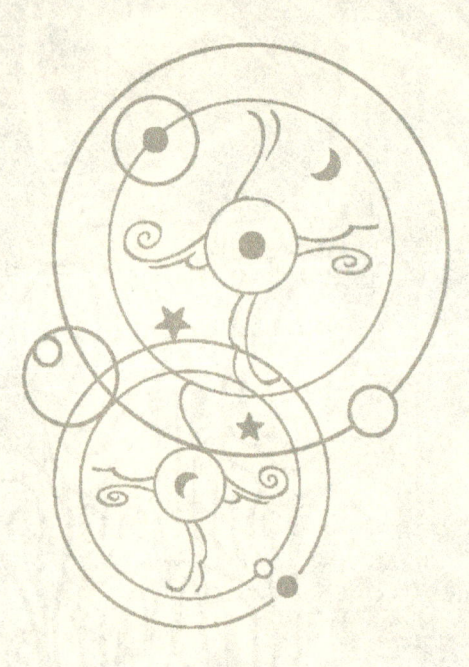

For 27 straight hours, I lay dreaming; I'd come upon one of these wretched creatures every hour or so. In dreamtime, each hour seems like a day unto itself. I conversed with these terrifying things in the dark, for they had secret words—with arcane meaning—to teach me, if I were to attain the true goal of my dream quest. I know not if these creatures, some no larger than children, others who were attempting to display their feminine charms & those that were outright brutes, wear their true forms; Or, if these are merely guises for the sake of my sanity. Though I guess these things would not hesitate to drive a man to madness, if one were not aware of the equations, or circles, of protection with which I'd been made privy to. I can feel it in my heart of heart, that these things are no wholesome things, indeed...

But! I have voyaged this far & the last of these...interdimensional beings... told me that there are only 4 more of their kind, who await me; The 4 Warlords, they've been called, again & again; Warlords of this netherworld on which I Drift. Should they let me continue upon my journey, they will lead me to & help me to pass through, the Gate to the Deeper Dimensions; Where, should it be fated, I will be granted court with The 7 High-Priests of Spawning Chaos. The gate itself is guarded by a ferocious quasi-god, known as The Stygian Abomination; A gigantic hydra, it's wizened babies' heads sprouting from the body of something that would most closely resemble a giant scorpion in our dimension. These great Warlords, each with a small squadron of their soldiers, will keep The Stygian Abomination at bay, as I dash off & away into another realm.

All of these different circles, these equations, were just a part of a bigger puzzle, though. I don't know if it was intuition, or dumb luck; but I began to see the bits & pieces I'd picked up along this dream quest, as fragments of a larger equation. The equations, the circles, were becoming more & more powerful; Magical! I could feel this in my heart of hearts & in the essence of my soul-stuff; What I knew to be some strange math—from inhuman minds—orbiting me in concentric circles or rings, many of them, rings of pure nuclear-fire. Numerals! I put my faith in these alien-spawned-equations; these protective rings, they became something not unlike circling, ethereal hornets, of such pure & Absolute Truth—

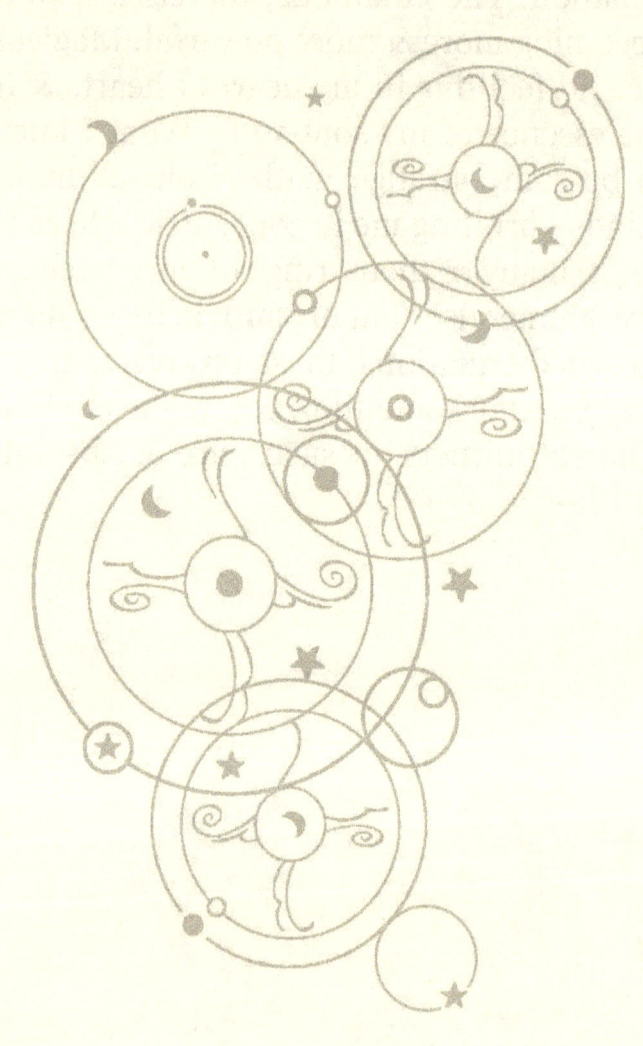

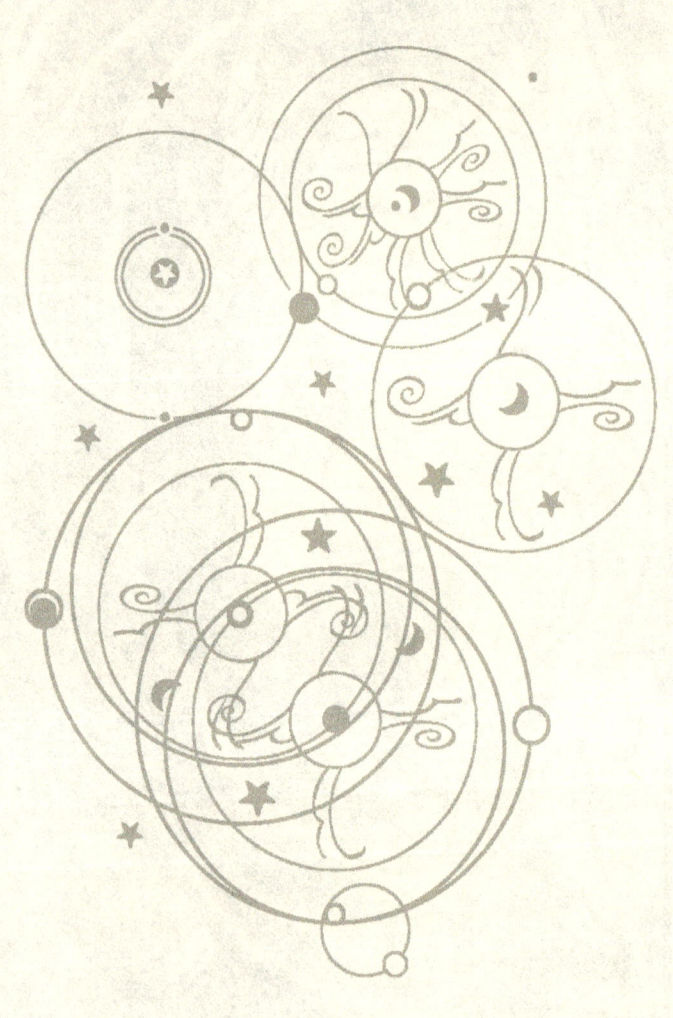

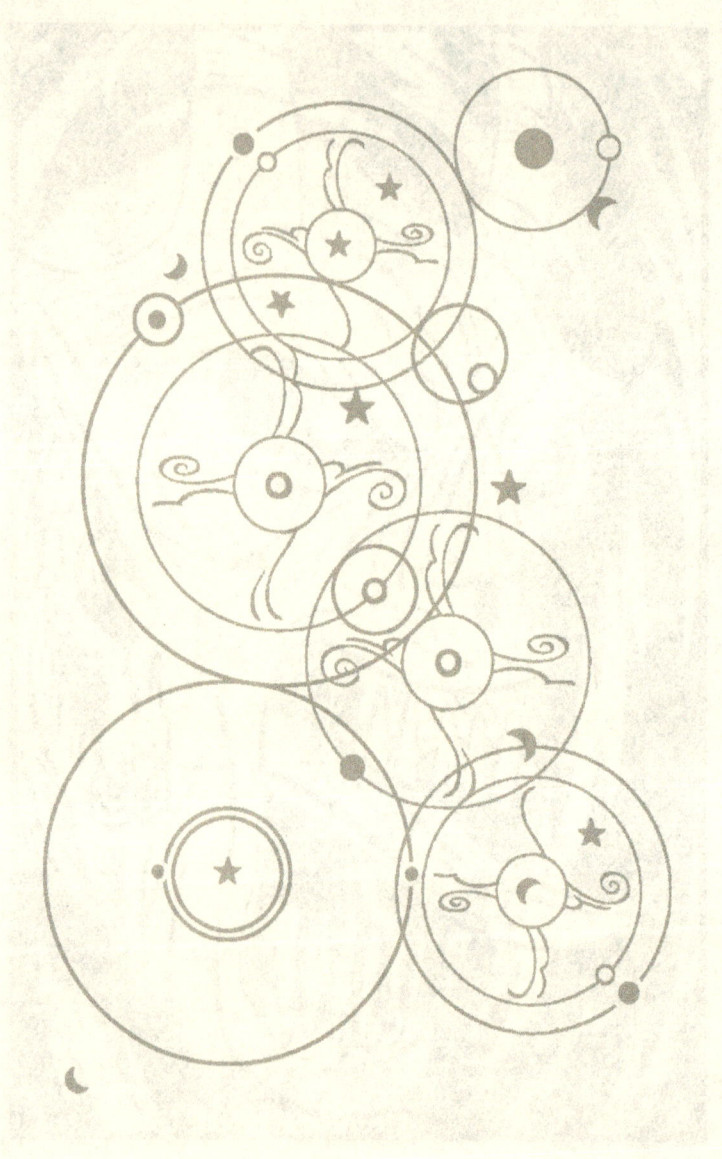

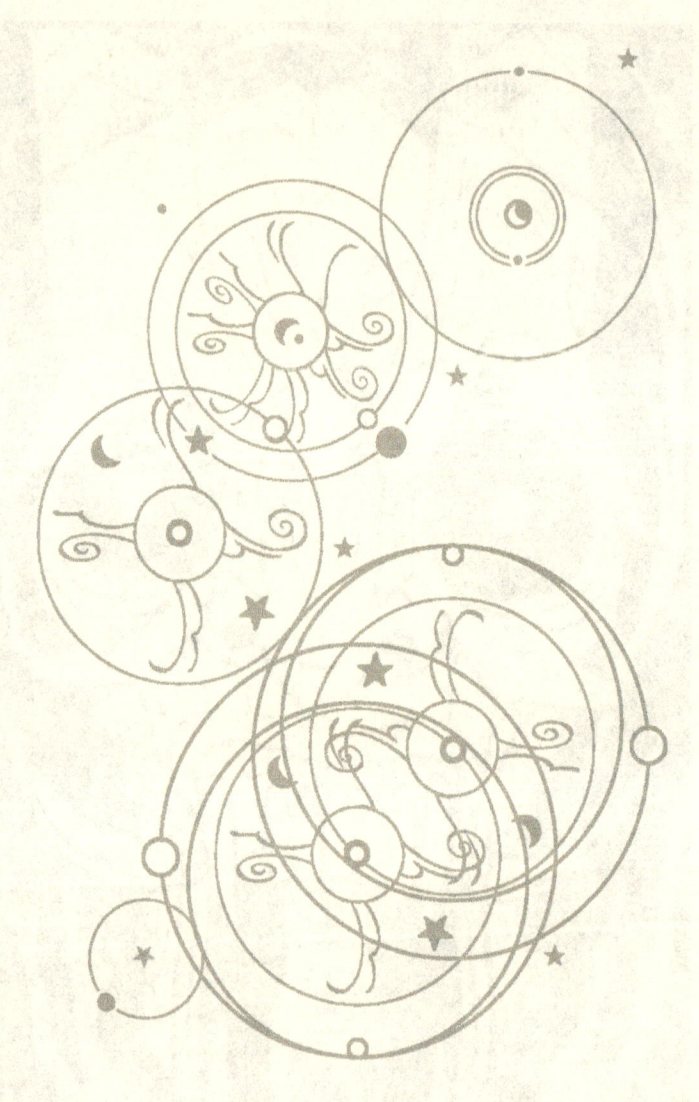

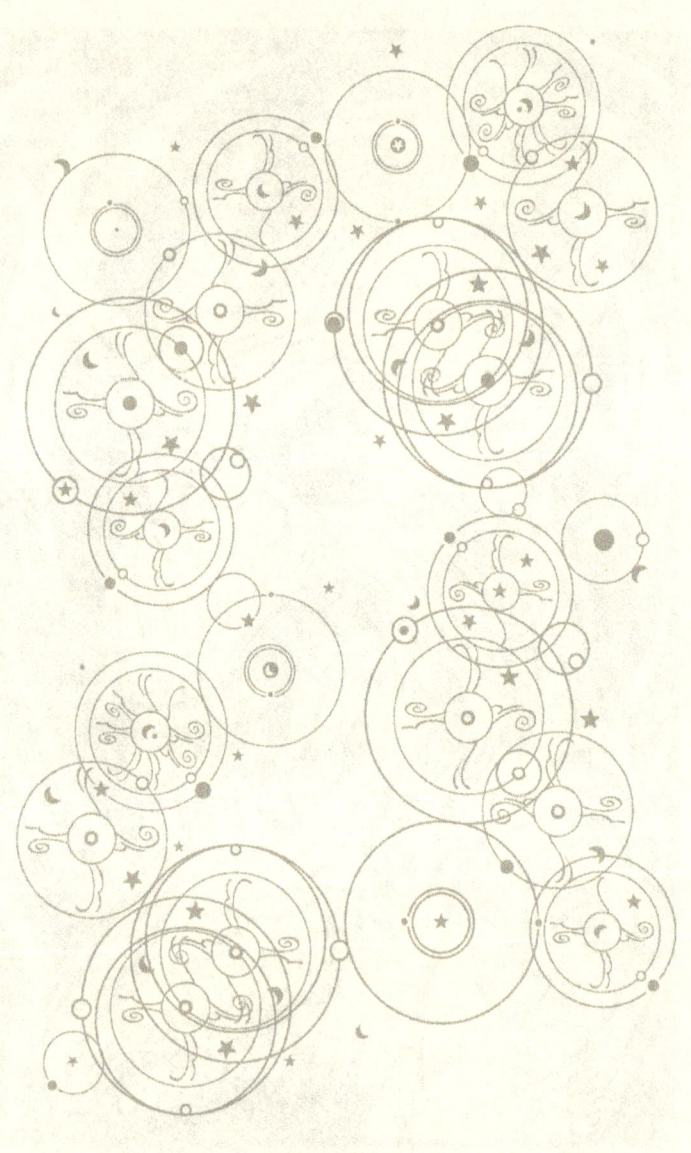

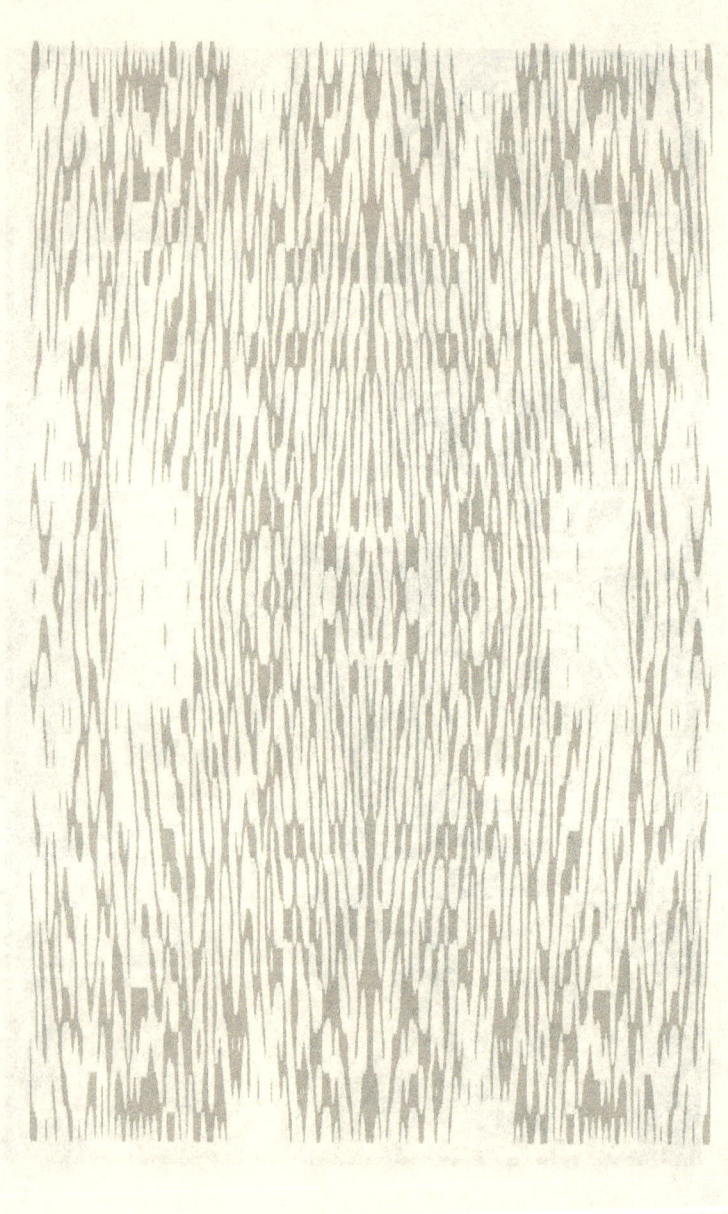

Eventually, I was permitted to enter the Veil of Spawning Chaos; One of the deeper folds in the fabric of the multiverse. I walked on 7 worlds over 7 hours, in that strange & haunted galaxy. On those worlds, I met with the High-Priest of each of these wicked & hostile planets. The Stygian Abomination, under the duress of The 4 Warlords of that disturbing nether-realm, telepathically sent me The Symbols of Names; Each name a key representing the secret, true name, of these Priest-Kings. Names that were like keys to their kingdoms & beyond...

If a Dream Traveler could palaver with all 7 of these Priest Kings, one could, potentially, find the power source of their devotion. This being One of The Lords of Outer Darkness...In this realm a great & terrible deity, a goddess! She was the inspiration for Hecate, for Shiva, for Kali, in our dimension, on our Earth; though none of those were her true name on this plane. Had I not been given The Symbols of Names, my mind would shatter when the High-Priests would each, eventually, utter one syllable of her name; which, when spoken aloud—I'd been sternly warned—was madness.

Before I am able to hold court with the Lord of Outer Darkness who rules this realm, I would first have to undergo a test, some horrible rite, which was performed by the 3 Guardians of Gt'rr'U'bhal; known collectively as Those Who Watch the Passageway to Her Lair.

I get ahead of myself, though, for even as I hope to leave that hopeless wasteland of a dimension behind me, I still have ways to Drift. I am in a tunnel, lit only in the deepest magenta light, the occasional violet colored lightning bolts swirling around the tunnel's circumference; this only helps enhance the strangeness of the entire situation. My soul-stuff is very near its point of exhaustion. I've never been away from my corporeal body for so long. I have a sudden fear of being mistaken for dead;

possibly even eaten by my cat, back on Earth—

Then, I come out of that whirling purple vortex, upon a plain of ruins. It was on this world, Dr'uhk B'ryn, that I came upon the first of these Priest-Kings; A creature shaped roughly like a human, standing nearly 15 feet tall; It's head, that of a carrion bird...It cried out, a massive cawing sound, "What errand do you have, and do you know my name? Tell me my name. If not, I'll eat you as a midnight meal!" Suddenly I was very glad I knew his symbol...

Having fulfilled The Obligation of Names, I was given the fortitude to withstand their abhorrent & ancient rite, as my consolation prize for surviving the whirlwind trips to 7 alien planets in the same number of hours. It was this rite that would allow me safe passage past Those Who watch the Passageway to Her Lair & into the heart of terrible Gt'rr'U'bhal. The Priest-Kings told me that it, the rite, would be exploratory in nature; of both the physical & the psyche; They warned that it wouldn't be pleasant at all. In fact, I'd been warned, it would be extremely painful & would seem to last an eternity. Then, as I began to despair! I remembered those equations, that nuclear-fire, the bright light of those circles! I couldn't physically see them, as I once had, but I felt their presence all around me. Through the ordeal, I was wrapped in the bright, white, nuclear-heat of their love...

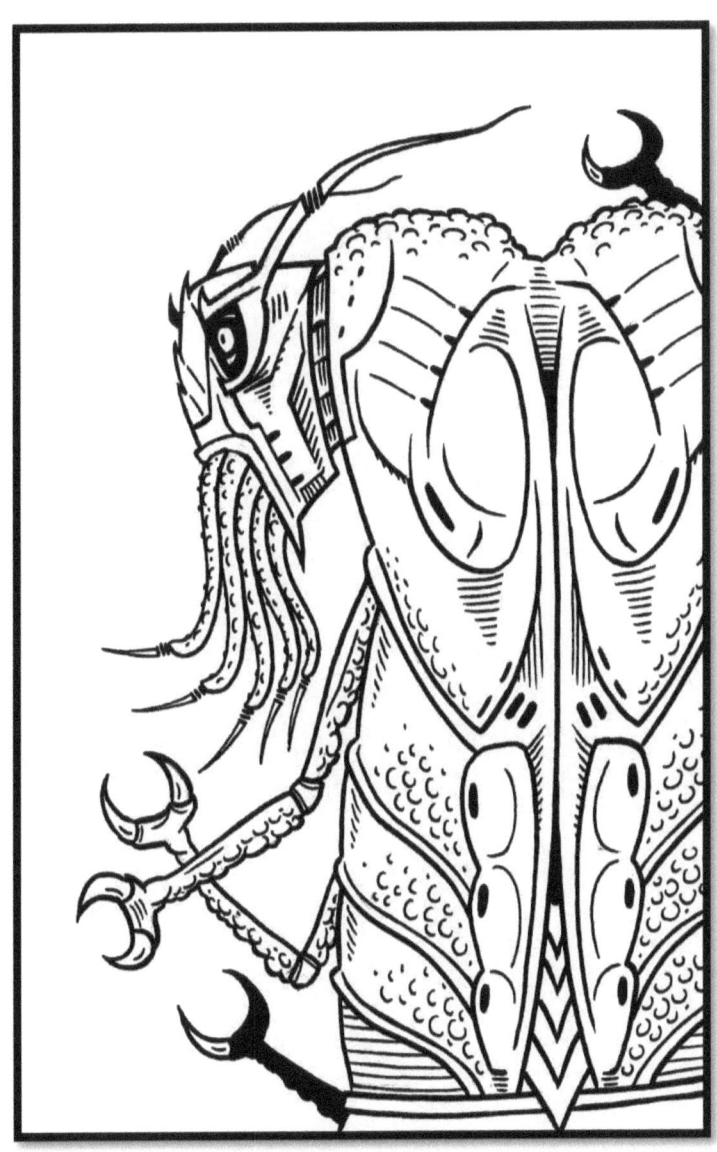

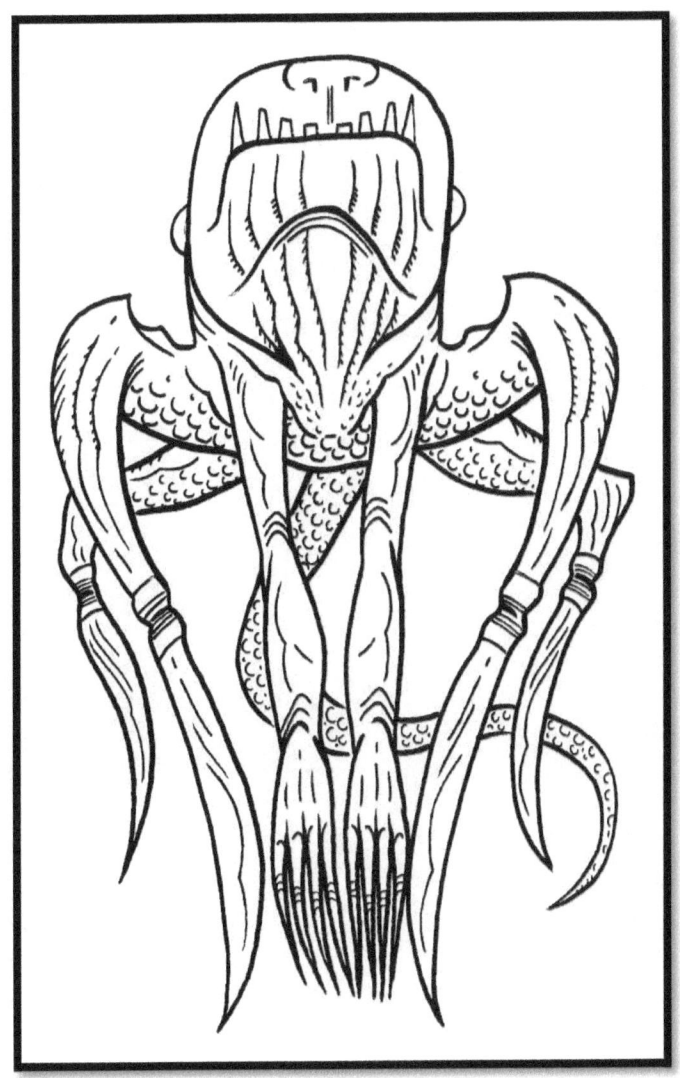

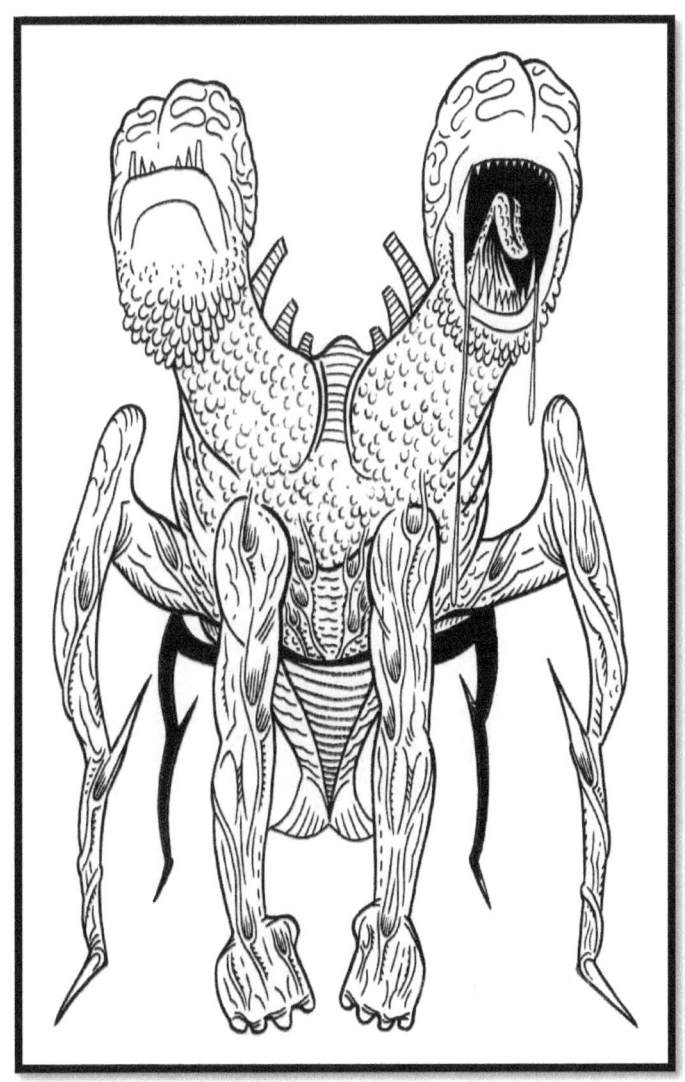

When the probing of Those Who Watch the Passage to Her Lair, those Guardians of Gt'rr'U'bhal, finally ended, I have never known such relief. I remember only flashes of those terrible things, those gargantuan creatures & worse, the acts committed to my soul-stuff. Thankfully, most of it was washed away in the heat of that nuclear-fire; the byproduct of the protective circles; equations of absolution. The parts I do remember, I will not speak of here...

But I am still whole. My soul weighed, much like those wizards of most ancient Aegypt. While not feather-light, my soul-stuff was deemed light enough to pass into Her Majesty's kingdom, Gt'rr'U'bhal...I quickly went Drifting down corridors, so large, so vast, there is nothing on our Earth to compare the height of those dark halls. The world's tallest skyscrapers; in cities like Dubai, Shanghai, or, Mecca, you may ask?

No. Not even those. These walls were carved, as far as the eye could see & despite the darkness of this place, I could somehow see very far, indeed. The carvings were of enormous landscapes, if galaxies could really be considered landscapes. The grim subjects of these alien bloody battle scenes, phantasmagorical, were what I perceived to be mighty battle-hosts. The armies of The Lords of Outer Darkness obliterating entire worlds. There were glyphs, 3 elephants high, written in characters sharing no geometry of anything on earth. To look upon them for too long made my soul-stuff nauseous, as if these symbols held the misery of every world The Lords of Outer Darkness had crushed beneath their forces of pure malice; of complete & utter hatred. As I was drifting down this cyclopean, eldritch hall, I became aware of some sort of distortion, black & strange, swirling in the path ahead of me. Then: "Who goes there?" a voice rumbled like an earthquake. Through that slowly crawling mist I made out, what I'd first assumed to be some colossal statue, barely move. "Frail human, go wander some other god's hall tonight, for to gain a visitation with...” The colossal creature spoke the true name of the goddess, its cyclops eye wreathed in flame. Back on Earth, while sleeping & Drifting, I'd plugged my ears. I screamed on that plane & on this one, too. The giant Cyclopean thing flapped its great leathery wings, the sound like great tree branches swaying & snapping in a heavy wind. The colossus lunged...

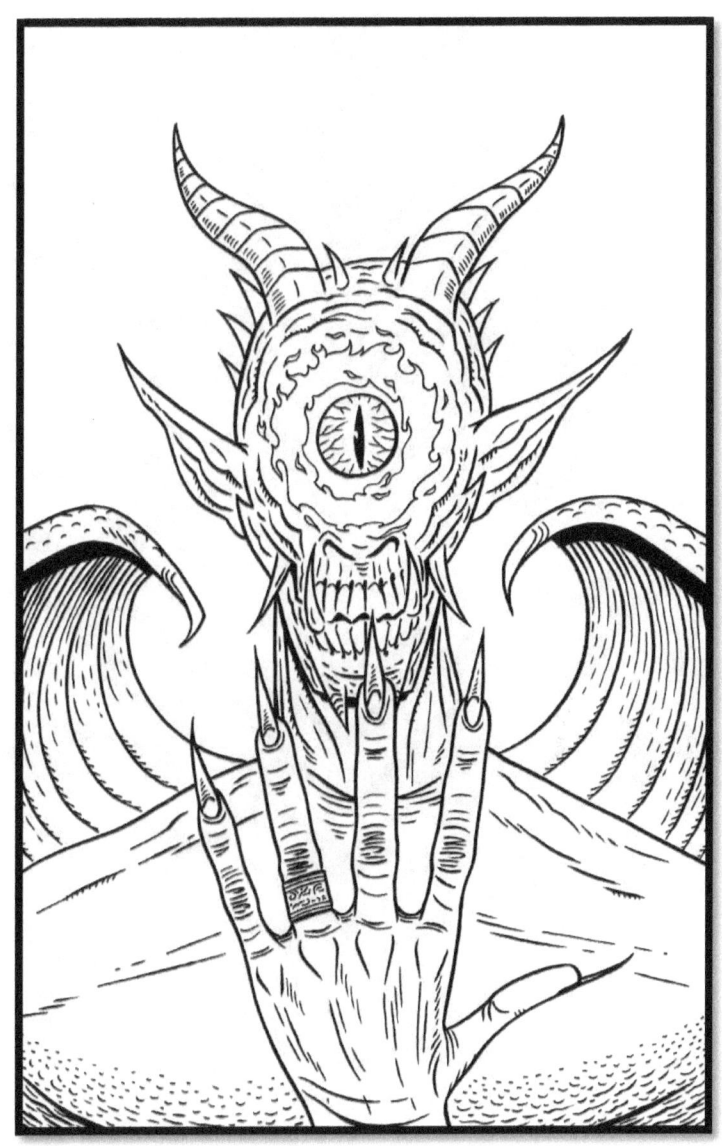

As the thing lunged, it had yelled, "Only by slaying me will you be granted audience with my Queen," the hideous creature was enormous & even in my soul-state, the psychic stench of the beast was unbelievable! As the shadow of the thing, larger than a 3 story building, fell down upon me, I had instinctually remembered all of the circles, all of the equations, I'd learned thus far in my voyage. I'd never done very well in Math classes, not even simple arithmetic, but somehow I miraculously piled all of those equations together, stringing them into something resembling some sort of an insane algebraic equation; one that would have taken up a city's block worth of chalkboard. Then, I'd solved it. At that moment the creature, the King of terrible Gt'rr'U'bhal, was incinerated in a blazing mushroom-cloud column of that absolute nuclear-fire. Instead of a crown, the demi-god (for he was not a true Lord of Outer Darkness) wore a band on his giant clawed finger, made of some xeno-forged iron. This ring was not a token of love, for that is a notion The Lords of Outer Darkness & their minions will never know, but instead, a token of servitude. The huge ring clattered to the alien flagstone floor Because in this realm, this was a game of chess. The King was merely a sacrifice, little more than a pawn, in fact. It was the Queen that ruled here; on the 17th planet from a nearly dead star, floating somewhere deep within the Gorgon system which is...nearly...some—

94546546846131466164646646465
46546546546541654654165466165879797
46431313134987946451654694131599465
46489786468465464646546846554 6465
46846546846515316549849492 49244464
42944944044460498498419849 8792949
49816510645184016161086165165 3165165
16516516510651651984091496404941561
08401864987498651651659859 49849865
13131458798496516516549784 986516516
54984986513216549841665498 41518494
98654165498645896418964986 48965498
64986498648964986415489645 6854986

5486419654695346598498654165324896
4518653411867842842842521313131131200
9494844049044940940160404604064464
6403165498798046510498299694974/8046
4084865148646848468486468868165164
5106418.1002...light years from the bright
& wholesome yellow sun of our own planet;
Earth. From the ashes of the incinerated
King, another strange curtain of oily black
mist, streaked with crimson lights...

When I came before that great and wrathful Queen, she had thanked me for slaying her cur of a husband...she'd told me that she had grown tired of her thrall, sick of his fawning ways. I wondered what the fawning of some dark, loveless, demi-god, would actually look like.

The Queen of this realm, The Realm of Spawning Chaos, asked what an insignificant mite such as myself was doing wandering so far from planet Earth. She stood stone still, her eyes glittering emerald & citron. This terrible goddess' voice was telepathic, for were she to speak, I would be shattered to smithereens. And still, this telepathic voice seemed even worse than death. It was as if I were drowning in pressure, the voice filling every space of my soul-stuff. Again, the all invading pressure, as her thought-voice assailed my being:

'Did you come to spawn with me little thing? To create offspring that can follow you back home, climbing and crawling from chaos, until finally emerging into your universe? To Earth? I've spawned with earthlings before,' even when her thought-voice tried to be persuasive, to coo, it was as though I were a drowning man being pushed under fathoms of ocean, crushed, 'I could transform myself to a size that even you could handle.'

This creature, this goddess, the inspiration for all of the Earth's most venomous & ruthless goddess deities—Hecate, Shiva, Kali...currently stood nearly as tall as I imagined the Empire State Building might be.

"I've come to learn the secrets of Anti-Matter. Dark Matter. I've come to harness the powers of black holes. I've come here, because I watch far too much news on T.V. That's a television, Oh Great Queen, and I watch humanity committing atrocious acts against one another, in the name of gods that are supposedly loving gods. And I know...that should my fellow man but see this account & realize that there are truly malevolent forces between the folds of reality, that surely they would realize—that perhaps most gods are, in reality—quite bloodthirsty things. I would bring this power of the voids back, and then I would make myself a necromancer, forcing the people of Earth to denounce their archaic gods, and worship the true source of absolute order. Mathematics! I will be to Anti-Matter, to Dark Matter, what J. Robert Oppenheimer was to the Atomic Bomb! I didn't travel for a tryst with a goddess, I assure you. I came for your key. I came to collect your equation, to draw your circle when the stars are right, to at least be able to rip a hole in the fabric of our universe, so that *we*, are sucked into *your* universe. The weird Universe of Dark Matter! I stand before you, after all these trials and tribulations, which in itself alone, proves that I am worthy! Please, Oh Mighty Queen, Keeper of the Knowledge of Gt'rr'U'bhal, who is Herself One of The Outer Lords of Darkness, I implore, I beg of you...Bestow me the knowledge of one of your great & terrible secrets of wrath! Speak your name!

She told me her equation, her name, but she spoke the numbers from her lips; blasting...blowing...rending my soul-stuff apart, with the hurricane force of her voice. I awoke in a wretched state, my dream quest lasting for 52 hours. My spirit had been roaming free of my body for over 2 days. I was sick as a dog for 3 days after the Drift...another 5 to recover fully.

No matter how hard I try, though, I can't recall those numbers that the Queen of Gt'rr'U'bhal spoke aloud, I can't even draw a representational circle of it; which is probably for the best. Because...until humans—different races, different creeds & religions—start loving one another, or at the very least respecting each other? I just might be tempted to use it...

This image of Artist/Author, Mat Fitzsimmons, was taken by his wife Brandi, moments after emerging from a 52 hour 37-minute trance-sleep. Just moments after his awakening at home, in Santa Cruz, Brandi reported his mad raving & ranting, his weird mutterings, about; Hecate & Shiva; Kali & Gorgons & J. Robert Oppenheimer; all of these, between an insane stream, thousands of numbers long, like some sort of an incantation. Numbers that both he & she have now forgotten. Mr. Fitzsimmons refuses to sleep without his wife & his 19-pound kitty-cat, Chloe, nestled by side–

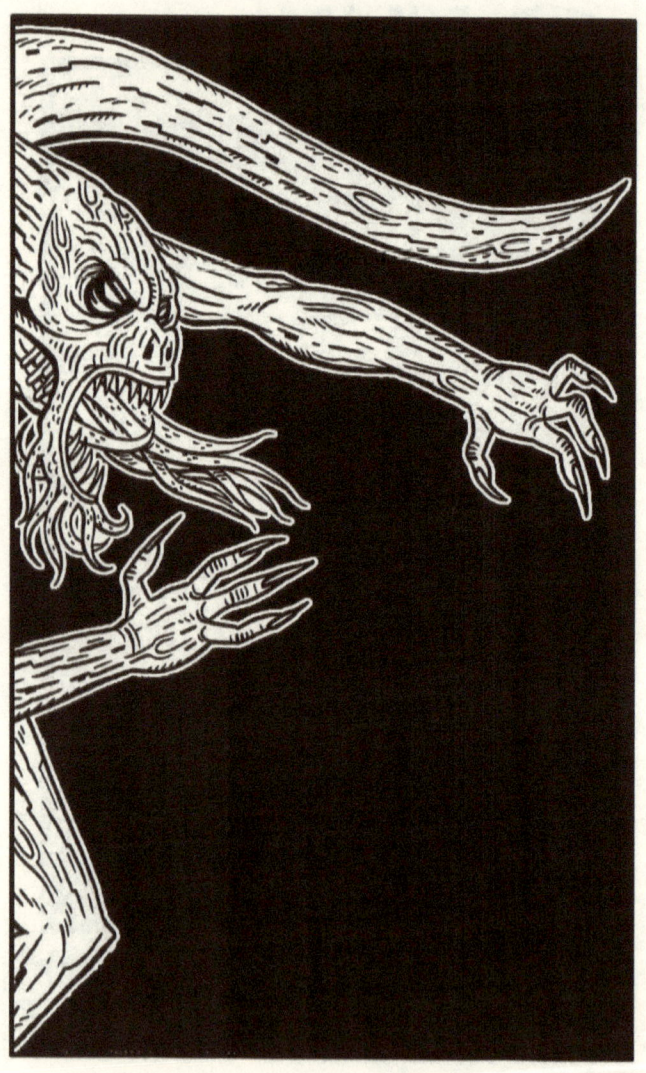